# GHOULIA

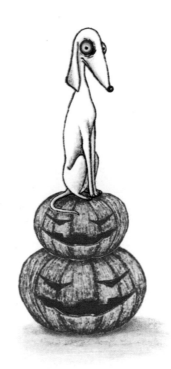

# GHOULIA

## Book 1

By Barbara Cantini
Translated from the Italian by Anna Golding

Amulet Books
New York

Cataloging-in-Publication Data has been applied for and may be obtained from the Library of Congress.

ISBN 978-1-4197-3293-5

Text and illustrations by Barbara Cantini
Original Italian title: *Mortina*
© 2017 Mondadori Libri S.p.A.
Translation by Anna Golding

Book design by Angela Jun

Printed and bound in China
10 9 8 7 6 5 4 3 2

Amulet Books are available at special discounts when purchased in quantity for
premiums and promotions as well as fundraising or educational use.
Special editions can also be created to specification.
For details, contact specialsales@abramsbooks.com or the address below.

Amulet Books® is a registered trademark of Harry N. Abrams, Inc.

**ABRAMS** The Art of Books
195 Broadway, New York, NY 10007
abramsbooks.com

To my family
—B. C.

Making friends can
be scary . . .

if you're a zombie.

# The Residents of

GHOULIA

AUNTIE DEPARTED

TRAGEDY

# Crumbling Manor

SHADOW

UNCLE MISFORTUNE

GRANDAD COFFIN

Ghoulia was no ordinary child. She didn't feel particularly different, but compared to other children, the color of her skin was a little odd.

She was pale, deathly pale: a greenish-gray color. Her eyes were as big and round as Ping-Pong balls, with bright purple shadows underneath. Purple was Ghoulia's favorite color.

Oh, and one last thing: Ghoulia could pull off parts of her body whenever she wanted, as if they were jigsaw puzzle pieces. Ghoulia was a zombie—a perfectly normal zombie girl.

So to Ghoulia, her life seemed perfectly normal.

She lived in Crumbling Manor with her Auntie Departed. There were lots of rooms where she could play whatever and whenever she wanted. The manor was surrounded by a huge garden with trees that were perfect for climbing. However, Ghoulia always made sure not to be spotted by anyone.

The nearby village

Ghoulia's best friend was an albino greyhound named Tragedy, who played with her all day. Nobody was quite sure whether he was dead or alive. At night, he slept at the foot of Ghoulia's bed.

Ghoulia loved her dog and her house and her family. But . . . there was a "BUT."

My great-grandparents

Me

One of my Auntie's hats (she has a million)

My favorite bow

The thing that Ghoulia wanted more than anything else in the world was to make friends with the other children in the village, but this was absolutely not allowed.

Whenever the children played near Crumbling Manor, Ghoulia spied on them. Sometimes, they were curious enough to peer through the manor's gates. But no one had ever been brave enough to enter the grounds.

*I wonder why*, thought Ghoulia.

Auntie Departed had made Ghoulia promise to *never* let herself be seen by anyone from the village, especially not by the children. Auntie worried constantly that they would be discovered and chased out of their home. Then where would they go? What would become of them?

One morning, Ghoulia had a brilliant idea:
"I will disguise myself as a normal, living child!"
She let herself into Auntie Departed's bedroom. She
borrowed Auntie's makeup, brushes, and hairpins.

Ghoulish Glow powder

Auntie's
hairpins

Then she dug out some brighter clothes from the old, dusty wardrobe.

A spider visiting from the attic

Granny Coffin

Very fancy gloves

Lots of my old relatives

Auntie Departed's cat, Shadow

Finally, Ghoulia waltzed down the staircase to show off her new look and ask, "Now can I go and play with the other children?"

Auntie Departed screamed and fainted. When she came to, she was furious with her niece. She explained that Ghoulia looked nothing like a normal child. Once again, Auntie Departed forbade Ghoulia from setting foot outside the manor.

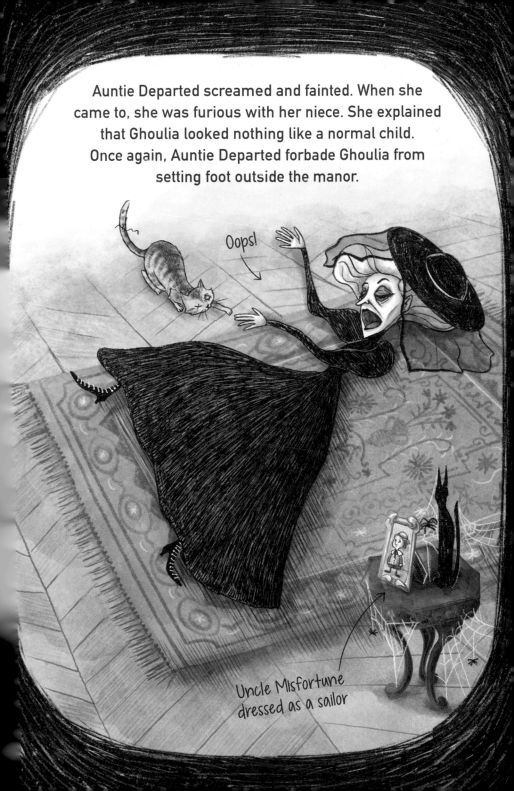

Oops!

Uncle Misfortune dressed as a sailor

Ghoulia followed Auntie's rules, and she didn't venture beyond the manor's walls. But one day, while she was spying, she heard the children talking about a night when they would all dress up as monsters and walk from house to house asking for a "trick" or a "treat." It was called "Halloween"!

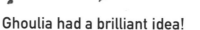

Ghoulia had a brilliant idea!

She would sneak out of Crumbling Manor on Halloween night dressed up as a monster! Then she could join in the celebrations with the other children.

# The (really) brilliant idea:

1  Do lots of research before the party.

2 Choose the perfect costume:

Ⓐ

Ⓑ

Consult Tragedy—he is very trendy!

Hmm . . . not a witch. Maybe I should just stick with being a zombie?

4 Find a suitable basket for the treats.

3 Create a distraction so that Auntie Departed doesn't notice anything. EUREKA!!! I'll unstitch Shadow—that way, she will be busy putting him back together.

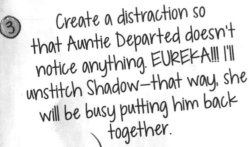

5 Get ready and go!

In the village, preparations for Halloween were underway well before the big day. Pumpkins of all different shapes and sizes appeared here and there, carved with silly or spooky faces.

The children added finishing touches to their scary costumes and chose the biggest possible baskets for collecting treats.

Meanwhile, back at Crumbling Manor, Ghoulia was extremely excited. All day, every day, she talked to Tragedy about Halloween. She yammered on so much that Tragedy couldn't take even the shortest nap. Days passed, and Halloween finally arrived.

A coat made out of Bigfoot fur (I don't think that I'll wear it; it's not very flattering.)

Ghoulia spent all day getting ready. Tragedy did her hair and checked that the shadows under her eyes were really, really purple.

Tragedy is an excellent hairdresser. He trained in Paris!

The only thing that Ghoulia still needed was a basket for the sweets. What could she use?

She could use Auntie Departed's jewelry box! She sneaked into her Auntie's bedroom, found it, and dumped out all the jewelry. Now, this wasn't exactly an ordinary jewelry box. It was Uncle Misfortune's head! And it would be difficult to keep him quiet. Ghoulia's uncle was a real chatterbox.

Eight-year-old Auntie Departed

Uncle Misfortune as a young man

Auntie Acid, Auntie Departed's sister

Auntie Departed's walking stick

Uncle Misfortune loved being left to snooze on top of the dresser, and he enjoyed chatting with the photo of his younger self hanging on the nearby wall. When Ghoulia disturbed him, he was in a very bad mood indeed. "What on earth is going on? Put my hat back on right away—I'm cold!" Ghoulia explained that she needed to borrow his head for the evening and promised that she would return him to his place on the dresser the next day.

**Achoo!**

Promise number 1

"If you come along and, more importantly, if you keep quiet for the whole evening, I will dust you for a whole year. And I'll bring you fat little worms to say thank you. Do we have a deal?" asked Ghoulia. Uncle Misfortune reluctantly agreed.

Promise number 2

VERMIS SOCIALIS:
A kind of worm. A typical pet kept by zombies. It's very tricky to track down worms who will put up with Uncle Misfortune. After a few days, they always sneak away.

Auntie's backstitch technique . . . I've never learned how to do it–it sounds boring.

Finally, Ghoulia was ready. She sped down the stairs looking for Auntie Departed and found her sitting in the parlor, trying to stitch up Shadow. She thought his tail had come unstitched during his nightly excursion around the manor grounds.

But Auntie Departed, having run out of gray thread, was stitching him up with thick, bright-orange thread.

Shadow's new bright-orange thread

(Shadow doesn't love his new look)

Painting
of
Grandad
Coffin

At the same time, Auntie was playing a game of chess with Grandad Coffin. She was winning, much to Grandad's disappointment. Ghoulia, taking advantage of Auntie's distraction, casually told her that she was off for a walk. "Yes, yes, of course!" her Auntie replied, waving Ghoulia away with a flick of her hand.

Ghoulia sped away from Crumbling Manor with Tragedy and Uncle Misfortune's head. She ran along the path, out through the gates, and off down the road that led to the village, as happy as could be.

Before long, Ghoulia came across a group of children dressed up in monster costumes. They were going from door to door asking "Trick or treat?"

Ghoulia was feeling a little shy, but she was willing to do anything to make new friends. So she said hello and asked if she could join their group.

The children looked at Ghoulia curiously. They were very impressed by her incredible head-shaped basket—it looked real!—and the strange dog walking by her side.

"What's your name?" asked the Witch.
"Ghoulia," she muttered quietly, embarrassed.
"Julia, what about your dog? What's his name?" asked the Wolf.
"Tragedy. He's an albino greyhound," Ghoulia answered.

Ghoulia explained that she had just moved to the village, and the children welcomed her to the neighborhood. Ghoulia's heart swelled with happiness. She set off with her new friends as they made their way down the lane.

R.I.P.

A real witch's cat

"We should sing a spooky song. Does anyone
know any good ones?" asked the Vampire.
"I do," replied the Mummy. He started singing, and
little by little all the others started to join in . . .

It was a dark, cold, rainy night
The sound of the wind gave a terrible fright
A strange graveyard at the end of the street
Where no living soul would expect to meet
An odd figure wand'ring 'round
Grave after grave in the muddy ground
Auntie Ann's ghost could sometimes be seen
Making sure all the tombstones stayed clean!

AUNTIE
ANN

After the song ended, Ghoulia exclaimed, "What a coincidence!
Just the other day, my Auntie Departed was giving her grave a
good cleaning. She loves keeping everything nice and tidy!"

The Witch chuckled, "Julia, you are really funny!" Then all of
the children joined in the laughter.

The children debated which of them had the scariest costume and how cool it would be to meet a real monster.

Ghoulia couldn't have been happier. These children weren't afraid of vampires, ghosts, or zombies. They even had a competition to see who could make the scariest face.

"I am a vampire—look
at my pointy fangs!"
hissed Michael.

"I am a witch—look at
my disgusting warts!"
cackled Theresa.

"I am a wolf-man—look
at my sharp claws!"
growled Johnny.

Ghoulia, too excited to remember
she was supposed to be an ordinary child,
demonstrated her special scary move.

ABRACADABRA!

She tossed her head into her hand, spun it around,
bounced it in the air, and finally caught it.
"I am a zombie—ABRACADABRA!!!"

The children fell silent. Ghoulia froze, realizing that she had given herself away.

Everyone stared . . .

. . . and stared . . .

. . . and stared.

Then Johnny, the youngest child of the group, broke the silence by yelling, "This is the most INCREDIBLE THING in the entire UNIVERSE!!!"
"You're a REAL ZOMBIE!!!" he shrieked.

"Yes—and I meant to say, my name is Ghoulia, *not* Julia!" She giggled.

"HOORAY FOR OUR FRIEND
GHOULIA!" they all shouted,
giving her a big hug. If she could
have, Ghoulia would
have blushed bright red.

From that day onward, the children started visiting Crumbling Manor. Finally, Ghoulia could play with her very own group of friends, and she only had to be herself.

In the end, even Auntie Departed was happy, because Choulia asked the village children to keep her secret. They agreed and made a pact between the members of the "Monster Society." To make it official, they performed a wild dance under the moonlight in Crumbling Manor's garden.

But reader, don't forget:
It's a secret, so keep your lips sealed!

Turn the page for some special, spooky Halloween fun!

# Here's what you'll need to dress up like Ghoulia at your next Halloween bash:

- White face paint or face powder
- Purple eye shadow
- Black lipstick
- Black wig
- Purple barrette
- Purple dress
- Black-and-white striped tights
- Black shoes

Get a parent, grandparent, auntie, or uncle to help you
put the whole look together and—*ABRACADABRA!*—you'll
look as fabulous as Ghoulia herself!

# Ghoulish Halloween Treats

## Ghoulia's Purple Punch

Purple is Ghoulia's favorite color, and this simple, sweet punch is her favorite drink to share with her friends. Try preparing it for your next Halloween party!

Here's what you'll need:
- ½ gallon red grape juice
- 2 liters lemon-lime soda

Get a parent to help you mix it all together in a large pitcher or punchbowl and serve over ice. Enjoy!

# Uncle Misfortune's Mud Mix

Uncle Misfortune likes keeping worms as pets—they make for great company! *Gummy* worms, however, make for great snacks. Ask a parent to help you create this special treat to share with your friends.

## Ingredients
- Chocolate pudding cups
- Oreos
- Gummy worms

Step 1: Remove the lids from the chocolate pudding cups.
Step 2: Mix 2 crumbled Oreos into each pudding cup.
Step 3: Top each treat with 3 gummy worms.
Step 4: Dig in!

# Ghoulia's

Which of these images of Ghoulia does not match the others?

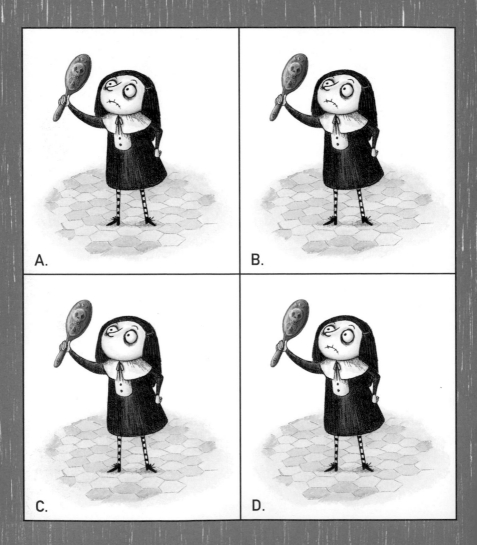

A.

B.

C.

D.

# Guessing Games

Which of these images of Tragedy does not match the others?

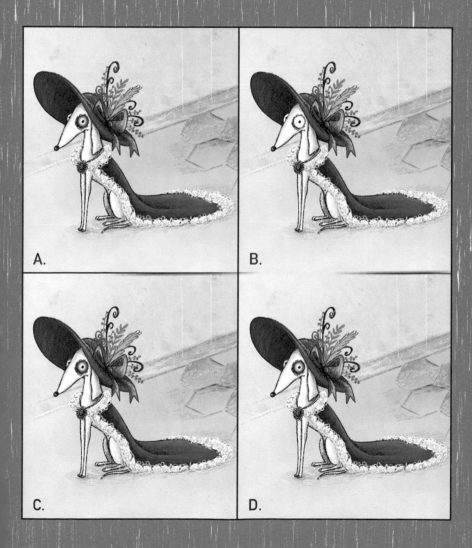

A.

B.

C.

D.

Which of these images of Theresa does not match the others?

A.

B.

C.

D.

# HAVE NO FEAR!

Ghoulia will soon return
for another adventure.

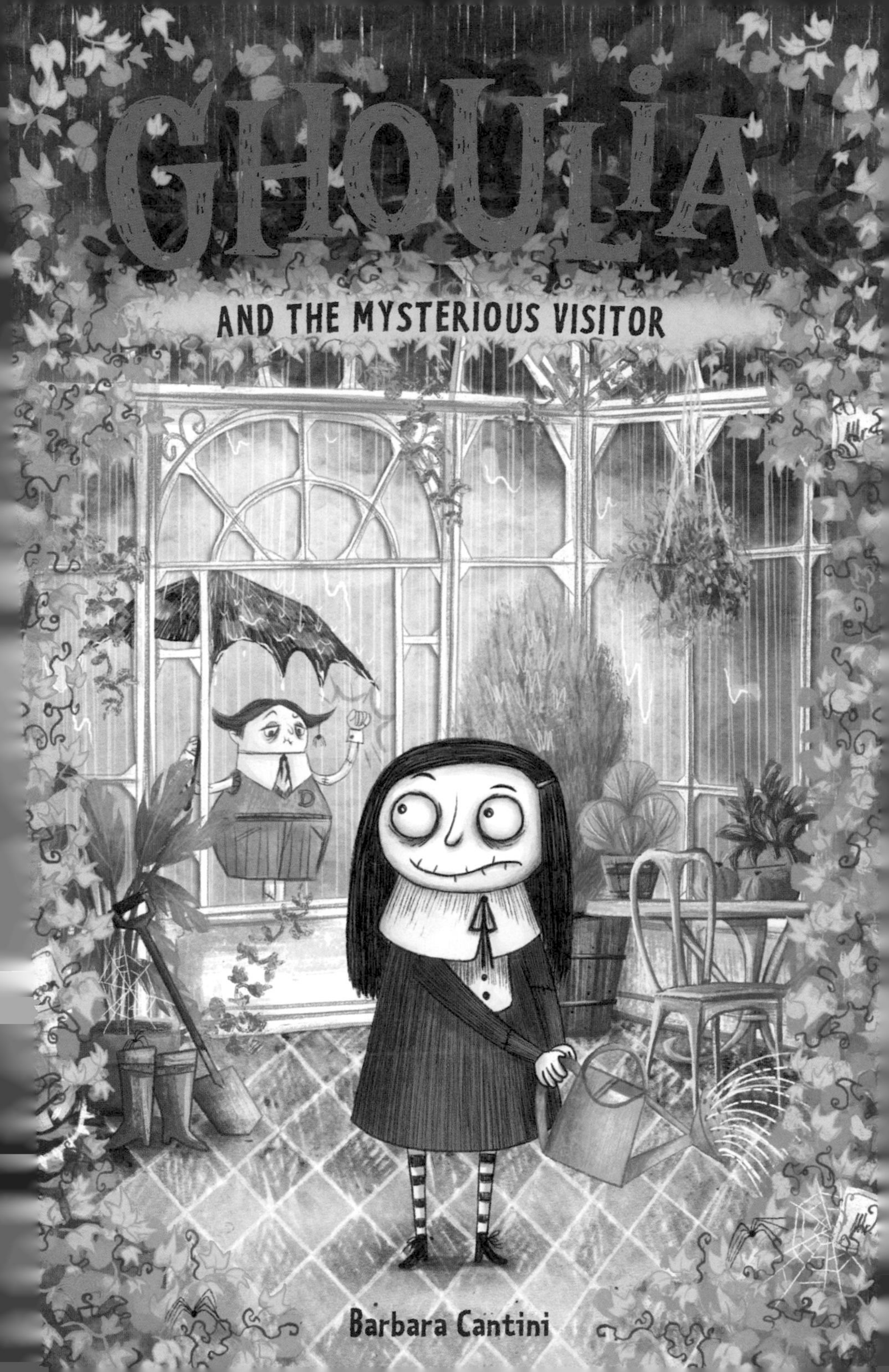
GHOULIA
AND THE MYSTERIOUS VISITOR
Barbara Cantini